I FELL IN LOVE

This book is dedicated to all children.

I FELL IN LOVE

Written by Ruby V. Shaffer

Illustrated by Jasmine Mills

Printed in the United States of America

Library of Congress Catalog Number: 2020901643

ISBN: 978-1-7331857-3-8

I fell in love the other day.

It was a great experience I must say.

It's an encounter we should all embrace.

Yes, everyone in the human race.

I fell in love with a book!
Come explore with me and let's take a look.

On this journey I'll take my twin.
She's my sister and my friend.

We're going to explore the deep blue sea.
It's smaller than an ocean, but big enough for me.

So close your eyes and let's take a dive.
We'll be in the sea by three and out by five.

Over to the left is a school of fish.
Sticking together they're less likely to become a dish.

My sister giggled when I said fish and school.
She said she wondered if they had to follow the rules.

Mammals such as dolphins, live in the sea.
But they come up for air to breathe,
Just like you and me.

Fish breathe under water using their gills.
So they don't need to come up for air,
And that's for real.

Some sea turtles are massive,
Like the leatherbacks.

They can weigh up to two thousand pounds,
Which I find is an interesting fact.

Corals are live animals,
And together they form coral reefs.

Just like trees form a forest,
Full of bright and colorful leaves.

Narwhals are the unicorns of the sea.
This is brand new news to me!

Their unicorn tusk is really a tooth.
It helps them catch fish
So it's put to good use.

Beluga whales grow long.

They say about fourteen feet.

They're called the canaries of the sea,

Because their sounds are so unique.

"Follow me," my sister said,
As she looked to the right.
What we witnessed going on
Was not a pleasant sight.

We saw a sea lion in a net,
That really looked distressed.
Most people are unaware,
That they caused this awful mess.

We carefully untangled the net,
And set the sea lion free.

I know animals don't smile,
But it looked that way to me!

Now you know why I fell in love,
With one of my favorite books.

What we experienced is more than reading
And now we're really hooked.

Tomorrow we're going to explore the sky,
The moon, and the stars.

And while we're on this journey,
We might just check out mars.

So fall in love with reading.
It's one of the best things ever.

Because what it's really meant to do...
Is to help you become more clever.

The End...No...A New Beginning

I FELL IN LOVE
Vocabulary Word List

awful: extremely bad or unpleasant

clever: intelligent and able to learn things quickly

distressed: feeling or showing extreme unhappiness or pain

embrace: to accept (something or someone) readily or gladly

encounter: an occasion when you deal with or experience something

experience: the process of doing and seeing things and of having things happen to you

explore: to travel over or through (a place) in order to learn more about it or to find something

giggled: to laugh in a nervous or childlike way

journey: an act of traveling from one place to another

massive: very large and heavy

pleasant: causing a feeling of happiness or pleasure

unaware: not having knowledge about something : not aware

unique: something or someone is unlike anything or anyone else

untangled: to separate (things that are twisted together)

witnessed: a person who sees something happen

Resource: Learner's Dictionary Merriam-Webster

Contractions

don't	do not
I'll	I will
it's	it is
let's	let us
she's	she is
that's	that is
they're	they are
we'll	we will
we're	we are

www.ingramcontent.com/pod-product-compliance
Lightning Source LLC
Chambersburg PA
CBHW041003170626
46815CB00002B/141